Edmat
5121
12/96
7.95

FANCY DRESS

Ray Gibson

Edited by Cheryl Evans Designed by Ian McNee
Illustrated by Chris Chaisty Photographs by Ray Moller

With special thanks to Eliza Borton, Johanna Briscoe, Jonathan Briscoe,
Matthew Evans, Ellie Gibson and Harry Gibson.

How to use this book

This book shows you how to make lots of different fancy dress costumes. Most of the costumes are based on clothes that you probably already have, such as T-shirts and sweatshirts. In this book these clothes are called basics. The ones that you need for each costume are shown in a list after the word **Basics.**
You alter the basics or make things to go with them to transform them into the costumes. The parts of each costume that you need to make are listed after the words **To make.**
The shopping lists on pages 28-29 tell you all the bits and pieces you need for each costume.

Contents

Clown

Basics: bright T-shirt; man's big, old trousers; bright tights; clashing socks; gym shoes or trainers; white gloves; any hat.
To make: bow tie; collar; hair; flower; buttons; braces. Find out exactly what materials you need for these on page 28.

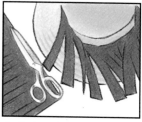

1. Snip along one long edge of tissue strips 20cm (8in) wide. Tape in layers into the hat, with a gap for the face.

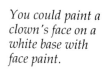

You could paint a clown's face on a white base with face paint.

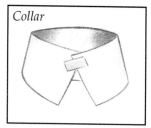

Collar

2. Cut a strip of white cardboard to fit your neck loosely. When you put it on, tape the top corners together.

3. Fold a big crepe paper bow. Add self-adhesive spots and stars. Fasten bow to collar with sticky tabs.

4. Cut a strip of stiff cardboard to fit inside the trousers' waistband. Tape or staple it into position.

5. Cut out and sew or stick bright felt shapes onto the trousers; or use any other bright scraps.

Two holes to sew them on with.

6. Cut two paper cups off about 1cm (½in) from the base. Poke holes in them with a sharp pencil.

Spread out the snips for petals.

7. For the flower, snip along a long piece of tissue paper 8cm (3in) wide. Roll it up and tape the end.

Tape green tissue paper leaves to your flower, if you like.

You could hold an eye-catching helium balloon.

Cut legs of old trousers off in jagged shapes.

Keep an eye open in charity shops for big, bright, old clothes. You should be able to find things that are not expensive.

The brighter the clothes you wear and the more they clash, the better your clown will look.

Putting the costume together

You will need someone to help you put this costume on. Put on the T-shirt, tights, socks and shoes first. Then follow these steps to put the rest together.

Pull the trousers on. Hold them up at your waist level. Ask someone to safety pin the ribbons to the waist at the back. Slant them inward.

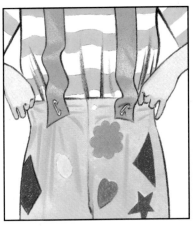

Cross the ribbons at the back and pull them over your shoulders. Pin them, the same distance apart as at the back, to the waist at the front.

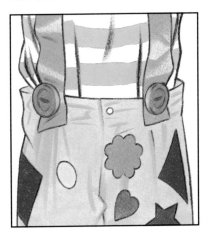

Paint the buttons brightly. Sew them on over the ends of the ribbons, through the holes. Use a darning needle and clashing yarn.

Put on the collar and bow tie so they hang loosely around your neck. Stick or staple the flower to the hat. Put the hat and gloves on last.

3

Black-and-white cat

Basics: black sweatshirt and thick, black tights, or black tracksuit bottoms; thick, white socks; white gloves.
To make: mask; bib; collar; tail; fish. Find out what materials you need on page 28.

Before you start

Cut wadding 19 x 23cm (7½ x 9in); fur fabric 70 x 20cm (28 x 8in) and another piece 40 x 10cm (16 x 4in). Put them aside and keep the scraps. Trace and cut out the cat mask template on page 32 in thin, black cardboard.

Mask

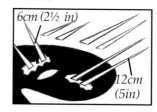

1. Cut whiskers in white cardboard. Do four long, thin ones and four short ones. Glue on, as shown.

2. Cut out the cheeks and brows in spare wadding. Turn over one of each shape to make mirror images.

3. Pinch and pull the wadding to fluff it up. Glue shapes over the whiskers to meet between the eyes.

4. Trace and cut out the ear patterns as described on page 32. Pin both to fur fabric and cut them out.

5. Tease out scraps of wadding and glue them down the middle of each ear, on the non-furry side.

6. Fold the ears opposite ways at the dotted line and staple. Staple the ears behind the mask, as marked.

Tail

Take the fur fabric 70 x 20cm (28 x 8in). On the non-furry side, put a lot of glue along a long edge. Roll it up longways from the unglued edge. Glue teased-out points of wadding to one end.

Bib

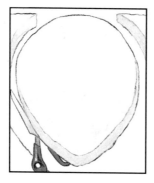

1. Draw lightly with a felt-tip pen, then cut out, a teardrop shape on the wadding 19 x 23cm (7½ x 9in). Fluff it out.

2. Glue more teased-out strips on top, down the middle of the bib. Safety-pin the bib to the sweatshirt from the inside.

Collar

When you are ready to put the costume on, turn the long edges of the fur fabric 40 x 10cm (16 x 4in) under, to fit the length of your neck. Wrap it around your neck and safety-pin at the back.

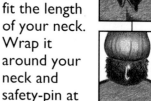

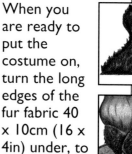

Fish

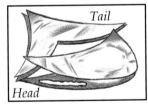

Draw, then cut, two fish heads and two tails in foil. Glue each pair together, with wadding in the head.

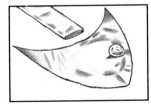

Glue foil balls on for eyes. Fold a foil strip 25cm (10in) long a few times as a spine. Staple on the head and tail.

Fold several strips of foil, each a bit shorter than the last. Fold them into a V-shape like this, for ribs.

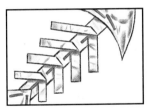

Staple them to the spine about 3cm (1in) apart. Put the biggest near the head, then in size order.

You could paint a black nose if you have face paints.

Glue sequins around the eyes to outline them, if you want to.

Add extra whiskers, if you like.

Put basic costume (except gloves) on first. Put on the mask and gloves last.

Thread elastic through elastic holes on mask, to fit around head.

Pin the tail on from the inside with two safety pins.

Attach tail to your wrist with elastic, if you like.

Tape a long thread to the fish head and tie the other end to your finger.

Wear thick, white socks rolled down to ankles.

Giant vampire bat

Basics: black sweatshirt, tracksuit bottoms, gloves, socks and gym shoes.
To make: wings; cap. See what you need to make these in the list on page 28.

To make the cap

Cut the legs off the tights. Put the top part on your head. Tie the ends with a rubber band and cut off any extra. Turn inside out. Trace the ear template (page 32) and cut two black felt ears. Stretch gently with your thumbs to hollow them out. Fold one side of each ear in as marked. Sew onto tights' waistband 10cm (4in) apart.

Wings

Follow steps 2 to 5 on the right to make the wing shapes for both costumes. Step 1 shows how to prepare a big, black plastic bag for the bat's wings. You use net for the butterfly's. See the page opposite for how to decorate the butterfly's wings.

Pull cap over ears to hide hair.

Buy plastic vampire fangs and a black eye mask from a joke shop, if you like; or paint them on with face paints.

Wear black socks rolled down, and black gym shoes.

Get help to tape or safety pin the straight edge of the wings along your arms and back from wrist to wrist.

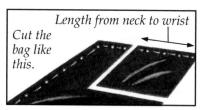

1. Lay the plastic bag flat. Cut off the sealed end. Slit up one side and flatten out the folds. Re-fold in half and pin.

Length from neck to wrist

Cut the bag like this.

2. Ask a friend to measure you from the base of your neck to one wrist. Cut the bag or net into a square this size.

Butterfly

Basics: pastel leotard or swimsuit; pretty, contrasting tights; ballet shoes or slippers.
To make: wings. See the list on page 28.

Wing decorations

Cut wings as for bat (steps 2-5, below) from one or more layers of pastel net.

Cut shapes from scraps (draw around a glass or plate for circles).

Pin shapes to the wings in a pattern that is the same on both halves.

Put a stitch in the middle of small shapes. Sew all around big ones.

Wind fluffy pipecleaners around a matching headband to make antennae.

Overlap the shapes on the wings, if you like.

Make or buy a pretty eye mask; or use face paint or make-up.

Hold the wings along your back and arms. Thread white elastic through the net at the elbows. Tie loops to slip over your arms. Do the same at the wrists, or use some double-sided tape.

Wear a shiny necklace or pretty earrings, if you like.

3. Fold the top right corner to the bottom left one and pin. Take the long, folded side to meet the left edge.

Long, folded side

4. Turn the plastic or net over. Pin the smaller top layer to the rest. Cut off the small triangle at the bottom.

Small triangle

5. Draw a curve between the corners of the short edge with a ballpoint pen. Cut off the curve and open out.

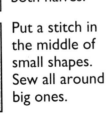

Skeleton

Basics: old, black, hooded sweatshirt; thick, black tights (or old, close-fitting tracksuit bottoms and socks); washable gloves.
To make: paint bones on clothes; chain. See list on page 28.

Paint a white face with black eye sockets with face paints, or put on a skull mask, before you pull the hood up.

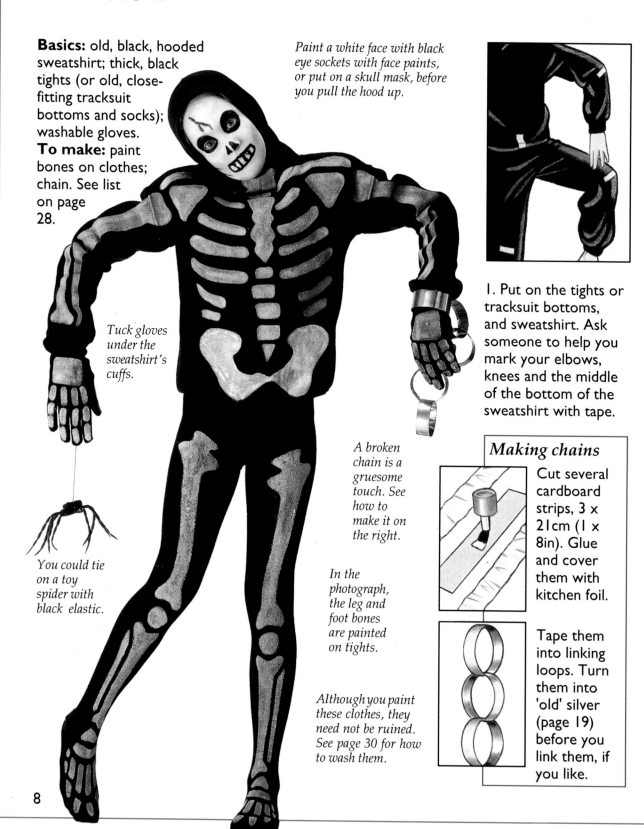

Tuck gloves under the sweatshirt's cuffs.

You could tie on a toy spider with black elastic.

A broken chain is a gruesome touch. See how to make it on the right.

In the photograph, the leg and foot bones are painted on tights.

Although you paint these clothes, they need not be ruined. See page 30 for how to wash them.

1. Put on the tights or tracksuit bottoms, and sweatshirt. Ask someone to help you mark your elbows, knees and the middle of the bottom of the sweatshirt with tape.

Making chains

Cut several cardboard strips, 3 x 21cm (1 x 8in). Glue and cover them with kitchen foil.

Tape them into linking loops. Turn them into 'old' silver (page 19) before you link them, if you like.

How to paint the bones

Mix white paint with a little water to make it creamy. Copy the shapes shown in this picture. Don't worry if they don't come out exactly like this. They will still look like a skeleton.

There is one upper arm bone.

There are two smaller bones in the lower arm.

Do a patch on top of the hand.

Lines of small blobs make finger bones.

Collar bone

Ribs

Spine

Pelvis. Put this on sweatshirt.

Thigh bone has lumpy ends.

Knees

There are two thinner bones below the knee.

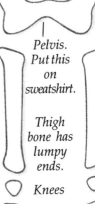

Make feet bones smaller and smaller nearer the toes.

2. Safety-pin the side edges of the hood under your chin so it fits snugly around your face. Take the shirt off and stitch the edges together with black thread.

3. Lay the sweatshirt flat. Roll up old newspapers to stuff in the sleeves. Press them as flat as you can. Fold newspaper to stuff inside the body too.

Remove plastic bag when paint is dry.

4. Lay the shirt on some newspaper. Tape it down to hold it in place. Paint the bones, as shown on the right, with a small decorator's brush.

5. Stuff the tights or tracksuit bottoms with rolled-up newspaper. Paint the leg bones as shown on the right. Start with the knees.

6. Paint hand bones on the gloves. Put a plastic bag on your foot, then the sock or tights foot. Paint the foot bones. Use the smaller paintbrush.

Boxer

Basics: plain, bright dressing gown (a silky one is good); shorts that match; black or white gym shoes or trainers, with white laces; sports socks; two bandages.

To make: belt; initials for robe. Look at the list on page 28 to see exactly what you need.

Add a trickle of blood if you have red face paint.

Put gel on hair and slick back from face.

Dab on grey, mauve and green face paint or eye shadow for a bruise.

Champion's belt

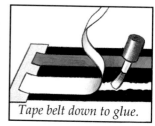

Tape belt down to glue.

1. Paint glue along the black cardboard. Press on the blue and white ribbons, as shown. Wipe off any extra glue with a dry cloth.

Stick shoulder pads in the robe, if you like.

2. When it is dry, staple the fringing or braid below the white ribbon. Cover the staples at the back with tape.

Wrap belt around waist and tape in position.

Robe

With a felt-tip pen, draw your initials on the felt squares. Cut out.

Cut a small felt square from the scraps, to go after each letter,

Stick to back of robe with double-sided tape.

Tape one end of a bandage to each palm. Ask a friend to wrap them tightly around your hands and wrists. Fasten with safety pins.

Twist strips of kitchen foil and glue them around the medal for decoration. Add extra twists and loops, if you like.

3. Paint glue thickly on the margarine lid. Press kitchen foil over it, tuck the edges under and fasten with tape.

Back-to-front person

4. Place the lid on top of your picture of a boxer. Draw around it with a pencil and cut out the shape.

5. Trim another ½cm (¼in) off all around your picture. Glue it to the middle of the lid, so the foil makes a frame around it.

6. Lay the middle of the belt over the lid (both face-down) and tape. Bend the ends of the belt up so medal lies flat when it is on.

This costume works best if you wear formal clothes because casual clothes look much the same from front and back. The same joke works really well for other costumes, too. Try a back-to-front monster (see page 22), for example.

Basics: shirt; tie; jacket; skirt; socks or tights and shoes.
To make: changes to mask. See page 28 for what you need.

Improving a mask

Lightly scratch the surface of a plastic mask with fine sandpaper.

Tape paper over the eye holes from behind. Paint eyeballs on the fronts.

Paint the cheeks, brows and mouth. Use paint and glue mixed.

For the best effect, hold your head back so the mask's chin stays down.

Glasses on the mask can add to the effect.

When you walk, your arms and legs seem to move in all the wrong directions.

Here you can see what the model looks like when she turns around.

Getting ready

Put a shirt, tie, jacket and skirt on back to front. You will need some help to button the shirt and knot the tie.

Put a face mask on the back of your head. Arrange hair around it so it looks natural. You could wear a wig if you like.

Headless man

See page 28 for everything you need, then follow all the steps on the next three pages.

Basics: black tracksuit bottoms; white T-shirt; black boots; brooch.
To make: head; shoulder frame; changes to big, old, man's, white shirt; boot tops; sash.

Shoulder frame

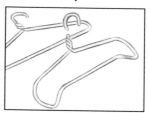

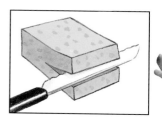

1. Pull a wire hanger into a rectangle. Bend the ends down. Twist to break off the hook. You may need adult help to do this. Bend the spike upright.

2. Wrap the spike in lots of tape. If your sponge is more than 2.5cm (1in) deep, ask an adult to slice it across with a knife to this thickness.

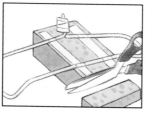

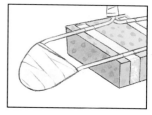

3. Lay the sponge under the hanger. If it sticks out more than 1.5cm (¾in), trim it with scissors. Tape it on well, right around the wire.

4. Tape a shoulder pad over each end of the hanger. Hang the shirt over the frame and tape the spike inside the collar strip, at the back.

5. Fasten the top buttons and put the shirt and frame over your head. Mark where your eyes are with felt-tip. Take off and cut out eye holes.

6. Crumple paper to fill the open neck. Gather the lace or doily and pin it on with a brooch. Dab the shirt with red paint mixed with glue.

To prepare the shirt

Bend the cardboard 60 x 5cm (24 x 2in) around to fit almost double inside the collar. Staple ends.

Make the shirt collar stand up and staple the points together. Snip the edge into jagged shapes.

Staple the ring inside the collar and cut off any cardboard that still shows above the jagged edge.

Cut off the cuffs and slash the ends of the sleeves.

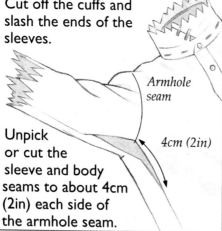

Armhole seam

4cm (2in)

Unpick or cut the sleeve and body seams to about 4cm (2in) each side of the armhole seam.

Put rubber bands over sleeves near wrists to gather.

Paint ragged ends of sleeves with 'blood'.

To disguise the eye holes, glue white net over them on the inside and paint with 'blood'. You will still be able to see.

Tuck tracksuit bottoms inside boots.

See how to make head on next page.

Wrap long piece of material, or long scarf, around waist and tie at the side for a sash.

Tape a long edge of the black material or felt inside each boot top. Then fold down to the outside.

To put it on

Put on the white T-shirt and tracksuit bottoms. Tuck T-shirt in.

Attach sticky tabs to the inside of the shirt, around the eye holes.

Fasten the top two shirt buttons. Put the frame on your head.

Fasten the rest of the buttons from the outside (or get help).

Press the sticky tabs gently to your face to hold in place.

Put your arms down the shirt sleeves. Cut seams more if you need to.

Tuck the big shirt neatly inside the tracksuit bottoms.

See next page for head.

13

Headless man's head

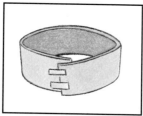

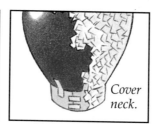

Cover neck.

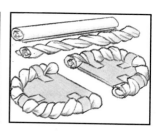

1. Bend the cardboard 8 x 40cm (3 x 16in) into a circle. Overlap the ends by 3cm (1in) and tape. This is the neck.

2. Blow the balloon up and knot it. Tape it, knot down, into the neck. Glue 3-4cm (1-1½in) squares of newspaper all over it.

3. Paint glue on top of the squares and add more until you have about four layers. When it is dry, cut the neck into points.

4. Cut two cardboard ears. Turn one over to make a left and a right ear. Twist pieces of paper to tape around ears. Tape the ears on.

Glue fringe of yarn for hair all around head.

Knot several long pieces of yarn together in the middle for moustache.

Short scraps of yarn for eyebrows and beard.

Do bloodshot eyes and pale, thin lips.

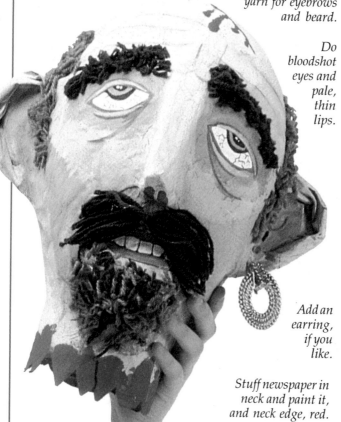

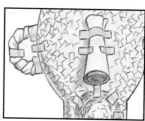

5. Crumple a little newspaper and wrap it in another piece to make a chin. Tape it to the bottom of the face, above the neck.

6. Roll up a strip of newspaper 10cm (4in) wide and tape it. Squash one end and tape it on for a nose. It may stick out.

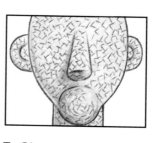

Add an earring, if you like.

Stuff newspaper in neck and paint it, and neck edge, red.

7. Glue more squares over the ears, nose and chin to hide the joins and attach firmly to the face. Use long strips over the nose.

8. When dry, pop the balloon. Paint head in skin tone. Add eyes and a mouth. Glue on hair and beard as shown on the left.

Scarecrow

For this scarecrow, collect all the things listed on page 28, then put them together like this.

Carrot nose

Make a cone from stiff paper, 18 x 26cm (7 x 10in). Follow steps 1-3 on page 24. Wind it tightly for a slim cone. Make holes for elastic to fit around your head. Paint it like a carrot.

Wear gloves.

Putting it on

Put on the T-shirt, trousers and jacket. Hold the trousers up with string.

Wrap a straw band (see above) inside each sleeve and trouser leg. Tie string around them.

Tape straw bands around the inside of the hat. Leave a space for your face.

Tie a bright scarf around your neck.

Put on carrot nose and hat last.

Follow steps 1-3 on page 24.

Straw bands

To make straw bands for the wrists, ankles and hat, sandwich pieces of straw between two lengths of tape.

Smudge your face with dirt. Or use face paints to paint it light brown with darker brown wrinkles.

Put a toy mouse or bird in top jacket pocket.

Knot string around trouser legs above knees.

Stuff a bright handkerchief in a side pocket.

Wear boots or old shoes.

Glue or sew bright patches onto trousers.

15

Superhero

This Superhero and the Superheroine on page 18 share many costume pieces. See how to make their belt, cuffs and breastplate here, and the cloak on page 19. Superhero also has a mask and Superheroine a headband. See page 29 for materials.

Basics: matching sweatshirt and tracksuit bottoms; trainers; thick socks.

To make: breastplate; belt; mask; cuffs; cloak.

Breastplate

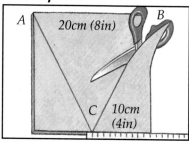

1. Cut a square of thin cardboard 20 x 20cm (8 x 8in). Mark half way along one side (C). Draw lines, then cut, from A and B to C.

Letter cut out.

2. Cut a piece of thick cardboard 9 x 8cm (3½ x 3in). Draw your initial really big on it and cut it out. Cut out the middle of the letter, too.

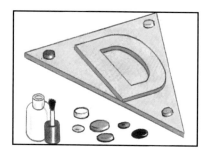

3. Glue the letter onto the breastplate, like this. Glue on small things, such as buttons and bottle tops, in a pattern and let it all dry.

Press into all the shapes.

4. Cut a piece of kitchen foil bigger than the breastplate. Cover the breastplate with glue and press the foil over it. Start in the middle.

5. Rub all the flat parts with a soft cloth to smooth and polish them. When it is dry, trim the foil to overlap by about 1cm (½in) all around.

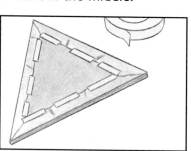

6. Turn the breastplate over. Fold the edges of the foil to the back and tape down. See how to give the foil an 'old' silver effect on page 19.

Find out how to make the cloak on page 19.

Wear thick socks that contrast with the basic outfit. Roll them down to your ankles.

All these accessories have been given the 'old' silver effect (see page 19).

See how to put on the whole outfit on page 19.

Superhero's mask

Trace the mask template on page 32 onto thin cardboard 30 x 9 cm (12 x 3½in). Cut it out, glue and cover with foil. Make snips in the eyes, fold flaps to the back and tape. Add elastic (page 30).

Making the belt

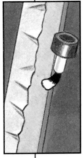

Cut a piece of thin cardboard 80 x 7cm (32 x 3in), and foil 1cm (½in) bigger. Glue the cardboard and stick on the foil Fold the overlaps back and tape.

Cut a small, cardboard triangle, add a cardboard initial and cover with foil, as for the breastplate. Glue it to the middle of the belt.

Cuffs

Cut here

Take thin cardboard 22 x 15cm (8½ x 6in). Cut one long side into a point. Glue, and cover with foil. Make two.

Superheroine

Basics: plain, bright swimsuit; clashing tights and long-sleeved T-shirt; contrasting knee socks; trainers or gym shoes.
To make: breastplate; belt; cuffs. (See how to make these three on pages 16-17.) Headband; cloak See page 29 for list.

Headband

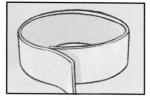

Take thin cardboard 9cm (3½in) wide and long enough to wrap around your head and overlap.

Mark the middle.

Point

Cut along one long edge to make the band narrow at each end and come to a point in the middle.

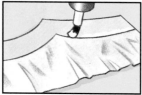

Cut the same shape in foil, but 1cm (½in) bigger. Glue foil to the cardboard, fold back the overlap and tape.

18

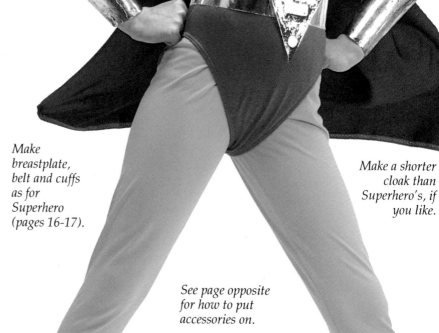

Wrap headband around head, overlap and tape.

Make breastplate, belt and cuffs as for Superhero (pages 16-17).

Make a shorter cloak than Superhero's, if you like.

See page opposite for how to put accessories on.

You could decorate your face with face paint or self-adhesive stars.

Scrunch your socks down to your ankles.

Wear the swimsuit over tights and T-shirt.

Cloak

Use silky material, 100 x 90cm (39 x 36in). Lining material is good. It is shiny and comes in bright shades, often 90cm (36in) wide.

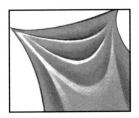

Twist rubber bands around two corners at each end of a short edge. Attach them about 12cm (4in) in. This gathers the cloth.

'Old' silver

Turn your accessories into 'old' silver by painting them with a mixture of black poster paint and glue that is not too thick.

When it is dry, rub as much black paint off as you like with a damp cloth. Your accessory will shine a duller silver, like old metal.

Putting on the costumes

When you put on the Superhero or Superheroine costume, put on the basics first. Tuck in Superhero's sweatshirt, and make sure Superheroine's tights and T-shirt are stretched smoothly under the swimsuit. Stick in the shoulder pads. Then ask someone to help you put on the accessories you have made, as shown in the pictures below.

Put the belt around your waist. Overlap the ends at the back and tape together.

Bring the ends of the cloak over your shoulders and safety pin to your chest.

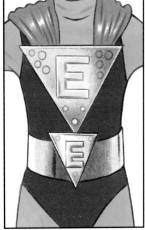

Place the breastplate over the ends of the cloak. Staple or sticky tab it into position.

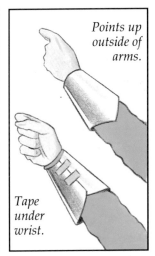

Points up outside of arms.

Tape under wrist.

Bend the cuffs around your wrists, overlap and tape. Put on the mask or headband.

More heroes

These costumes use the same accessories as the Superhero and Superheroine. You can change the shape of the breastplate and add new things, such as a mask, tunic or hood, for more hero characters, like these.

Space Lord and Ghostly Warrior

Basics: black sweatshirt and tights or tracksuit bottoms; thick black socks; black shoes.

To make: belt; cuffs; breastplate; cloak. (See how to make these on pages 16-19.) Tunic; mask for Space Lord. Tunic; hood for Ghostly Warrior. See what you need on page 29.

Paint a ghostly face.

Sling a toy sword in an extra belt.

Purple is good for the cloak.

Space Lord wears extra belt, black gloves and a ring of twisted foil.

Cut Ghostly Warrior's cloak and tunic into tatters.

Space Lord's Mask

Trace and cut out the shapes on page 31 in thin cardboard. Stick the flashes onto the mask, then cover with glue and kitchen foil with 1cm (½in) overlap to fold back. Add cardboard strips to go around your head.

Hood

Fold the short ends of the thin, black material together.

Staple along one long side, turn inside out, then put on your head.

Tuck the ends into the neck of the sweatshirt and ease into shape.

Tunic

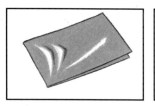

You need some silky material, twice as long as you are from shoulders to ankles and as wide as you are across the shoulders.

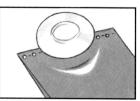

Fold the short sides together. Pin the fold. Place a small plate half on and half off the material, in the middle of the fold.

Draw around the half plate with a black felt-tip pen. Cut out the shape. Remove the pins. Try it over your head to see if it fits.

Mad scientist

Basics: old, white shirt your size; old tie; man's big, old, white shirt with pocket; plain, dark trousers; any dark socks and shoes; old spectacles.

To make: prepare the shirts and tie; experiment bottles; secret formula. All the things you need are given on page 29.

1. Cut off the collar, cuffs and bottom of the man's shirt, and the tip of the tie, in jagged shapes. Dab with black paint.

2. Snip black paper into a plastic bottle. Cut out a cardboard explosion with one extra-long point to go in bottle. Paint it.

3. Paint the inside of another plastic bottle green. Use paint mixed with glue. Tape a crazy, plastic straw into it.

Put gel on hair and twist into points.

Wear an old pair of glasses at a crazy angle.

Dab black explosion marks on your face and shirt with face paint or make-up.

Cut the trousers into rags, if you don't need them again.

Long strip of paper hangs out of pocket. Black felt tip figures and symbols make a secret formula.

Smear black paint on legs.

21

Space monster

Basics: big, old, black sweatshirt and tracksuit bottoms; black socks, gym shoes and gloves; any T-shirt.
To make: mask; tail; paint body.

Mask

Fold

1. Trace and cut out the shapes on page 31 in stiff, black paper. Paint a design on half the mask in dark green paint.

Both sides match.

To put mask on, hold it to your face and ask someone to bend strips around your head and tape at back. Put mask on last.

Find all the materials you need on page 29.

Wear black gloves.

For how to wash the paint off these clothes, see page 30.

For feelers, make holes through single sections of egg cartons. Poke pipecleaners through and bend to keep in place. Paint black. Twist other end around fingers.

2. Fold the mask along the fold line, press, then open out to blot pattern on both sides. Repeat with pale green paint. Do the same on the muzzle.

Changing shape

Put on a T-shirt. Hold sponges or egg cartons on your shoulders. Ask for help to tape them on as huge shoulder pads. Tape all the way around under your armpits.

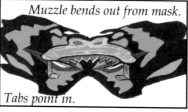

Muzzle bends out from mask.

Tabs point in.

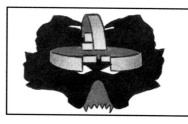

3. Outline one eye with red paint. Fold the mask to blot it on the other eye. Paint red teeth and nostrils on the muzzle. Let it dry.

4. Bend back the tabs on the muzzle and fold the ends under 2½cm (1in). Glue the ends flat onto the front of the mask, near the bottom.

5. Tape the strips of cardboard 4 x 30cm (2 x 12in) onto the back of the mask, like this, and make them curve back.

Body

1. Lay the sweatshirt on newspaper. Blot one half with dark green poster paint.

2. Quickly fold shirt in half from side to side. Press with a rolling pin. Repeat with pale green.

3. Do the same on the bottoms. Paint one leg, fold it on top of the other and press.

Tie tail to wrist with thread.

Tail

Cut off one leg of the tights and stuff with crumpled newspaper. Tie the open end with strong, black thread.

Mix green paint and glue on a plate. Press a crumpled rag into the paint and dab all over the tail.

Pin tail to back of trousers from the inside with a large safety pin.

Wear monster sweatshirt on top of T-shirt and shoulder pads.

Roll socks down.

Paint spikes black.

Cut a sponge into triangles for spikes. Glue and pin to end of tail.

23

Wizard

Basics: red tights, or tracksuit bottoms with red socks; red sweatshirt.

To make: tunic; hat; medallion; wand; hair; beard; moustache.

Tunic

Make a tunic in thin, red, material. Follow the steps on page 20, using measurements from page 29.

Hat

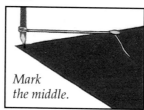

Mark the middle.

1. Tie string to a pencil and hold it at one corner of the red paper. Stretch and pin the string to the middle of a long edge.

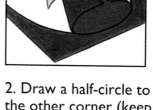

2. Draw a half-circle to the other corner (keep the string stretched). Cut it out. Bend the corners down toward the curved edge.

3. Overlap the corners until the paper forms a cone that fits your head. Paper clip together. Tape to hold.

4. On thin cardboard, trace and cut out the star on page 31. Fold the red, shiny paper into lots of layers.

5. Draw around the star onto the paper. Cut out the shape to get lots of stars. Stick them onto the hat.

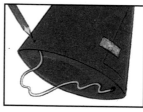

6. Poke holes at each side of the hat with a pencil. Thread with elastic to fit under your chin.

Wand

Roll the garden cane, or stick, in red foil paper. Glue or tape it on. Tape together lots of strips of gift wrap ribbon. Tape to one end.

Beard, moustache and hair

1. Cut wadding 19 x 23cm (7½ x 9in). Cut a teardrop shape out of it. Snip a curve in the top. Cut strips in it. Tease into points.

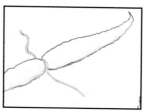

2. Cut more wadding 2 x 32cm (1 x 13in). Tie white thread around the middle. Tease the ends into points for moustache.

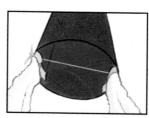

3. Cut two pieces of wadding 4 x 30cm (2 x 12in). Cut two thirds of the way up each. Tape in the hat 12cm (5in) apart.

To put on

Put on basic costume and tunic. Put sticky tabs on dry skin, as shown. Press on beard and moustache. Add the medallion and hat.

Medallion

Glue top of margarine tub lid and cover with foil. Trim to 2cm (1in), fold edges to back and tape.

Roll strips of foil and bend around the gumdrops. Twist ends together and snip off extra.

Glue the lid and press gumdrops on it in a pattern. Snip pieces of gumdrop to fill the gaps.

Paint thickly all over the lid with glue. It looks cloudy at first, but dries clear.

Twist lots of foil strips. Tape to the back, all around the lid. Bend into curly shapes.

You could make wadding eyebrows, too.

You could put wrinkles around eyes with make-up or face paint.

Stick extra stars to the strips on the wand, if you like.

Put wadding all around hat, if you want to.

Stick silver ribbon to back of medallion to hang around your neck.

You can stick medallion to tunic with sticky tabs to stop it from swinging.

Glue shiny stars or pin brooches to front of tunic, if you like.

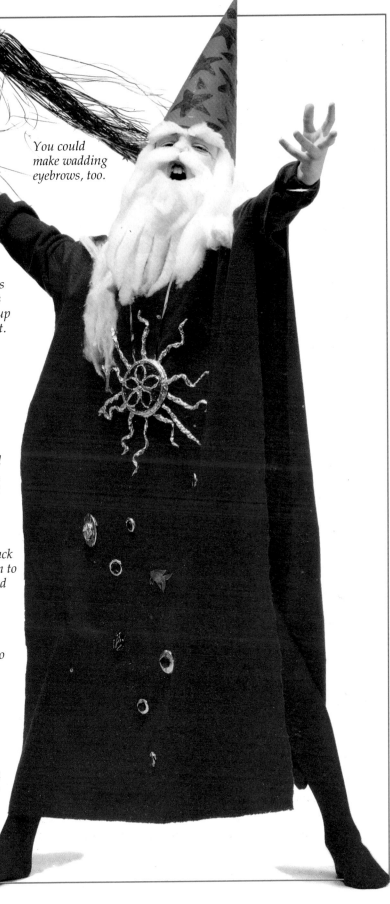

Comic waiter

This waiter has a magic tray that never spills, but people don't know that if you pretend to tip it at them.

Basics: black jacket and trousers; white shirt; bow tie; black shoes and socks; white gloves; large, white, cloth napkin.
To make: jacket tails; tray. See page 29.

Tails

Cut a long triangle of black material in half, like this.

Sew or staple the pieces to the back edge of the jacket.

Put all the basics on first. Put the bow tie and gloves on last.

You could paint on a curly moustache with face paint.

If you put a napkin on the tray, use an old one, as you have to glue it on.

You could use the same joke tray with a waitress's costume.

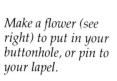

Ask someone to put sticky tabs on the gloved hand you want to hold the tray with. Get them to press the tray on firmly.

Make a flower (see right) to put in your buttonhole, or pin to your lapel.

To make the tray

Wash and dry half an empty egg shell. Paint it carefully inside and out with glue.

Stick the egg shell onto a plastic egg cup. Glue the egg cup to a paper plate.

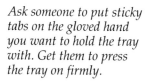

You can dip a white flower in red paint to dye the tips of the petals.

Gel hair and part in the middle.

Add light things to the tray, such as plastic cutlery and a paper napkin, if you like. A flower is a nice touch.

Pretend to trip and spill the tray. It will stay firmly stuck to your hand.

Carry the cloth napkin over one arm. Hold it there with sticky tabs.

The more horrified you look at 'spilling' the tray, the better the joke is.

Making flowers

Cut a long strip of tissue paper about 8cm (3in) wide. Snip all along one edge.

Roll up the strip and tape the end. Gently pull out and spread the snips for petals.

Make a slice of toast. When cold, cut into four, paint with glue and stick to the plate.

Put cornflakes into a paper bowl. Mix them with glue to stick them together.

Paint inside a clear, plastic glass with white paint and glue. Tape in a straw.

Glue the white cloth to the tray. Arrange and glue on all the things you have made.

Shopping lists

Check you have all you need from these lists before you start.

Clown p.2-3

Tape or stapler
Several bright felt squares
2 paper cups
Darning needle and bright yarn
4 safety pins
Sharp pencil
Two sided sticky tabs
2 pieces of wide, bright ribbon 1m (1yd) in length
White cardboard 45 x 7cm (18 x 3in)
Red crepe paper
Orange and another bright tissue paper
Self-adhesive stars and spots
Face paints or make-up
Basics: Bright T-shirt, man's big, old trousers, white gloves, bright tights, clashing socks, trainers or gym shoes, hat.

Black-and-white cat p.4-5

Greaseproof or tracing paper
Thin black fur fabric 70 x 30cm (28 x 12in)
Medium wadding 35 x 25cm (14 x 10in)
Thin black cardboard 23 x 15cm (9½ x 6½in)
Thin white cardboard 12 x 6cm (5 x 2½in)
PVA glue
Stapler
Scissors
Black face paint (optional)
Ballpoint pen, pencil, felt-tip pen
Dressmaking pins
8 safety pins
Strong black thread

Black shirring elastic 55cm (22in) and 25cm (10in)
Kitchen foil
Basics: black sweatshirt and thick tights or tracksuit bottoms, thick, white socks, white gloves.

Giant vampire bat p.6

Large, black plastic bag
Rubber band
Tracing paper and pencil
Tape measure
Dressmaking pins
Needle and black thread
Scissors, clear tape
Ballpoint pen
Black felt 24 x 28cm (10 x 12in)
Old pair of thick, black tights
Face paint or joke vampire teeth
Basics: black sweatshirt, tracksuit bottoms, socks, gloves and gym shoes.

Butterfly p.7

Dressmaking pins
Pastel net, the length you are from wrist to wrist with your arms stretched out to your sides, and 80cm (32in) long.
Scraps of silky material
Things to draw around, such as a plate or glass
Felt-tip pen, scissors
Fine white shirring elastic
Headband
2 fluffy pipe cleaners
Needle and thread
Face paints or make-up
Basics: pastel leotard or swimsuit, pretty, contrasting tights, ballet shoes or slippers.

Skeleton p.8-9

Black and white poster paint and thick brush
Small decorator's paintbrush
Old newspapers
Clear tape
Needle and black thread
2 large safety pins
2 small plastic bags
Thin white cardboard 3 x 21cm (1 x 8in)
Kitchen foil, PVA glue
Black and white face paints or skull mask.
Basics: old, black, hooded sweatshirt and tracksuit bottoms ironed flat (both to fit as tightly as possible), with socks; or thick, black tights; black, washable gloves.

Boxer p.10

2 squares white felt 10 x 10cm (4 x 4in)
2 small safety pins
Ruler, scissors, clear tape
Stapler, double-sided tape
Small margarine tub lid (any shape), kitchen foil
Thin black cardboard 80 x 6cm (32 x 2½in)
80cm (32in) blue ribbon and white ribbon, both 1cm (½in) wide
80cm (32in) gold or yellow fringing or braid
PVA glue and brush
Picture of a boxer
Black felt-tip pen, pencil
Clean, dry cloth, hair gel
Face paint or eyeshadow
Basics: plain, bright dressing gown, shorts to match, black or white gym shoes or trainers, white laces, sports socks, two bandages (any kind), shoulder pads.

Back-to-front person p.11

Face mask, optional wig
White paper, poster paints
Fine sandpaper
PVA glue, clear tape
Basics: Shirt, tie, jacket, skirt, socks or tights, shoes.

Headless man p.12-14

1 wire coathanger
1 pair shoulder pads
Foam bath sponge 14 x 11cm (5½ x 4in)
Stapler, PVA glue, clear tape, two sided sticky tabs
Red paint and paintbrush
Felt-tip pen, scissors
Thin cardboard 60 x 5cm (24 x 2in), 2 rubber bands
Piece white lace or doily
Long piece of narrow, material or scarf for sash
Man's big, old, white shirt
2 pieces black material or felt 52 x17cm (22 x 7in)
Old newspaper
For the head:
1 round balloon
Thin cardboard 8 x 40cm (3 x 16in), and 2 pieces 9 x 5cm (3½ x 2in)
Old newspaper, clear tape
Poster paints and brush
Brown or black yarn
Basics: black tracksuit bottoms, white T-shirt, black boots, big brooch.

Scarecrow p.15

Thick string
Bright scraps of material
Straw (from pet shops)
Clear tape
Sheet of stiff paper and orange poster paint
Shirring elastic
Face paints or make-up

Basics: T-shirt (any kind), large, old jacket and trousers, boots or old shoes, gloves, bright scarf and handkerchief, old hat, toy mouse or bird.

Superhero p.16-17

Coat lining material to contrast with basics, 100 x 90cm (39 x 36in)
25cm (10in) shirring elastic
Stapler, paperclips, PVA glue, clear tape
3 safety pins
2 small rubber bands
1 pair shoulder pads
Damp cloth, old saucer
Black poster paint and paintbrush
Greaseproof or tracing paper, pencils
Thin cardboard in these sizes: 20 x 20cm (8 x 8in), 80 x 7cm (32 x 3in), 15 x 15cm (6 x 6in), 30 x 9cm (12 x 3½in), two pieces 15 x 17cm (6 x 7in)
Thick cardboard 9 x 8cm (3½ x 3in)
Kitchen foil, scissors, ruler
Bottle tops, buttons etc.
Soft, dry cloth
Basics: matching sweatshirt and tracksuit bottoms, gym shoes or trainers, socks.

Superheroine p.18-19

As for Superhero, plus:
Thin cardboard 9 x 30cm (3½ x 12in)
Basics: plain, bright swimsuit, clashing tights and long-sleeved T-shirt, contrasting knee socks, trainers or gym shoes.

Space lord p.20

As for Superhero, plus: black coat lining material for the tunic: as wide as your shoulders and twice as long as from your neck to feet.
Small plate
Black felt-tip pen
Dressmaking pins
Thin cardboard 31 x 28cm (13 x 12in) and 2 strips 4 x 30cm (2 x 12in)
Kitchen foil
Basics: black sweatshirt and thick tights or tracksuit bottoms, black socks, gloves, gym shoes or trainers, leather belts.

Ghostly warrior p.20

As for Superhero, plus: grey coat lining for tunic (same as Space lord's)
Thin, black material 53 x 90cm (22 x 36in)
Face paints or skull mask.
Basics: as for Space lord, plus toy sword.

Mad scientist p.21

2 plastic bottles
Black felt-tip pen
Crazy straw
Piece thin, white cardboard, poster paints, PVA glue
Scraps of black paper
Long strip of paper
Face paints or make-up
Hair gel
Basics: old, white shirt to fit you, old tie, old trousers (not jeans), big, old, man's white shirt, old spectacles, dark socks and shoes.

Space monster p.22-23

Tracing paper and pencil
2 large sponges or cardboard egg cartons
Stiff black paper 38 x 50cm (16 x 21in)
3 pieces stiff, black paper 4 x 30cm (2 x 12in)
clear tape, PVA glue
2 paper clips
Green and red poster paint and big paintbrush
Old plate (to mix paint)
Rolling pin
For the tail:
Sponge
Old, thick, black tights
Old newspapers, rag
Strong, black thread
Large safety pin, sponge
For feelers:
Ten pipe cleaners
Ten cardboard egg carton segments
Black paint
Basics: T shirt (any kind), big, old, black sweatshirt and tracksuit bottoms (ironed flat), black gloves and long socks, black gym shoes.

Wizard p.24-25

Thin red material twice as long as you are from neck to feet and as wide as from elbow to elbow (hold your arms out to the sides to measure).
Medium wadding 29 x 32cm (11½ x 13in).
Stiff red paper 70 x 77cm (29 x 32in)
Pencil

Thin string 45cm (19in) long
70cm (29in) silver ribbon
Sheet red, shiny paper
Greaseproof or tracing paper
Scissors,
Thin cardboard
White thread
Garden cane or stick
Two sided sticky tabs, clear tape, PVA glue
Round plastic food tub lid
Kitchen foil
White shirring elastic
Large, red gumdrops
Roll of narrow, shiny, red gift wrap ribbon.
Basics: red sweatshirt, red tights, or tracksuit bottoms with red socks, glittery brooches.

Comic waiter p.26-27

Black material 42 x 44cm (17½ x 18½in) cut into a long triangle
Hair gel
Face paint or make-up
Sheet bright tissue paper
Sticky tabs
Black thread and a needle, or a stapler
For the tray:
Square of white cloth, or old, cloth napkin, to cover the tray, and hang over
Paper plate and bowl
Plastic egg-cup
Transparent plastic glass
Straw
Egg shell, slice of bread, cornflakes
White paint, PVA glue, clear tape
Basics: black jacket and trousers, socks and shoes, white shirt and gloves, bow tie on elastic, white cloth napkin (for over arm).

29

Templates

Templates are shapes you draw around. You need to trace them from the book to use them. Some are whole templates and some are half templates. You trace these in different ways, which are explained here.

Usually, you transfer the shapes onto paper or cardboard, as described in the steps here; but sometimes you use the shape as a pattern. This means you cut it out and put it on top of material or paper, pin it on or draw around it, then cut the shape out. It tells you on the template if you need to do this.

To trace half templates

 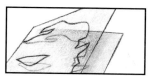

1. Fold tracing paper in half, then open it. Put it over the template, with the crease matching the edge of the page. Trace the shape.

2. Take the tracing off and re-fold it. Turn it over. Draw over the outline you can see to complete the shape. Open out, then follow steps 2 and 3 below.

To trace templates

1. Put tracing paper over the template. Hold in place with paper clips. Draw over the outline with a soft, dark pencil.

2. Turn the tracing paper over. Put it on the cardboard you are using and go over the shape again with a hard, sharp pencil.

3. Go over the faint lines this leaves with pencil (use a white crayon on black paper or cardboard). Cut out the shape.

Washing clothes

If you paint clothes that you want to wear again, let them soak in cold water. This helps lift paint out of them. Rinse and squeeze out. Then wash in a machine as usual. Do not mix paint with glue if you want to wash it out.

Eye holes

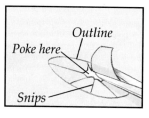

Outline
Poke here
Snips

Poke a pencil or pen into the eye hole. Put a scissor blade into the hole and make snips to the eye outline. Cut around the outline last.

Elastic holes

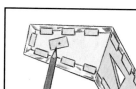

Make small holes with a sharp pencil. They will be stronger if you put a small square of tape over them, then pierce again. Thread elastic.

Press the pages as flat as you can to trace over the fold in the middle.

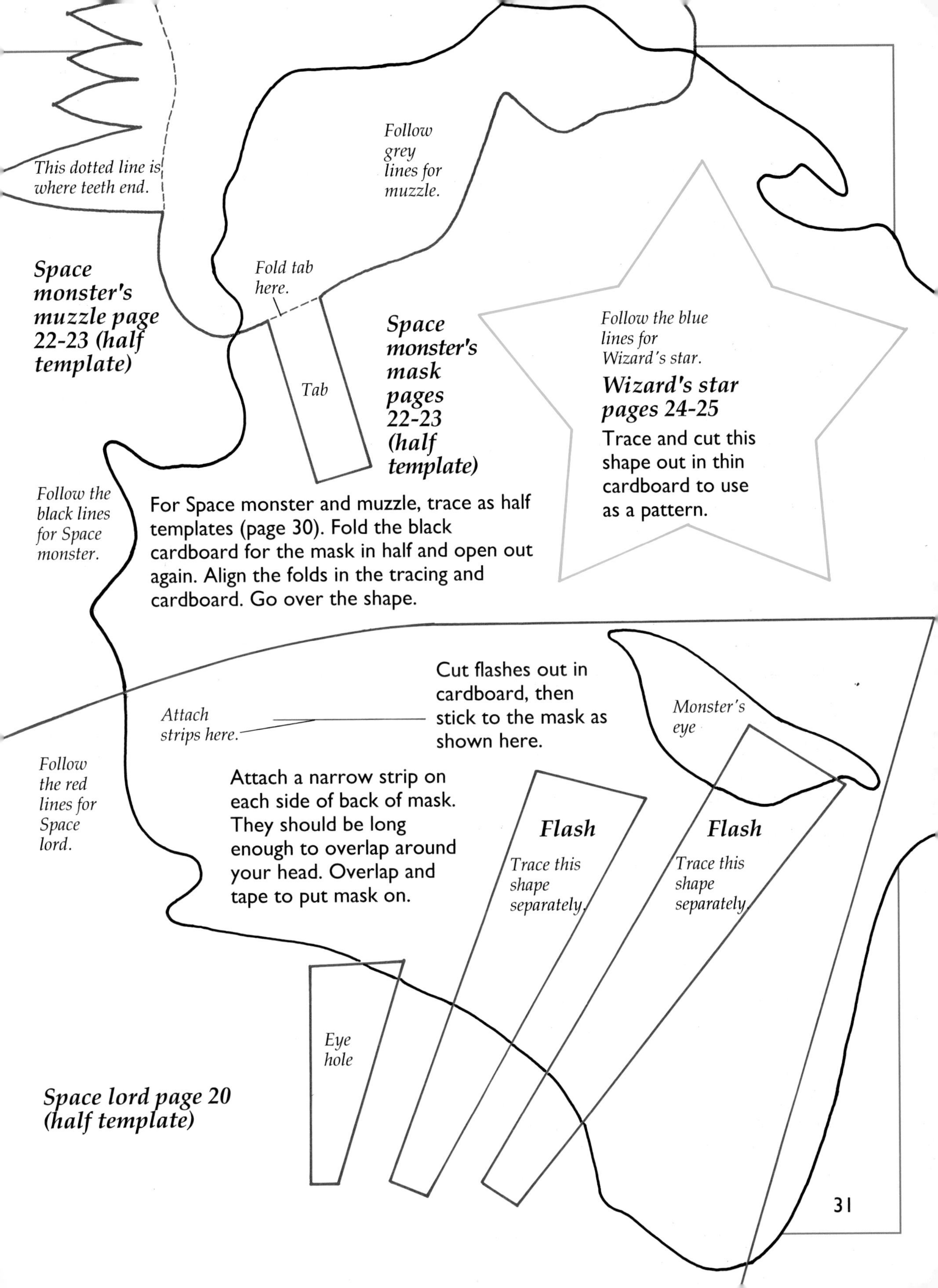

This dotted line is where teeth end.

Follow grey lines for muzzle.

Space monster's muzzle page 22-23 (half template)

Fold tab here.

Tab

Space monster's mask pages 22-23 (half template)

Follow the blue lines for Wizard's star.

Wizard's star pages 24-25

Trace and cut this shape out in thin cardboard to use as a pattern.

Follow the black lines for Space monster.

For Space monster and muzzle, trace as half templates (page 30). Fold the black cardboard for the mask in half and open out again. Align the folds in the tracing and cardboard. Go over the shape.

Attach strips here.

Cut flashes out in cardboard, then stick to the mask as shown here.

Monster's eye

Follow the red lines for Space lord.

Attach a narrow strip on each side of back of mask. They should be long enough to overlap around your head. Overlap and tape to put mask on.

Flash

Trace this shape separately.

Flash

Trace this shape separately.

Eye hole

Space lord page 20 (half template)

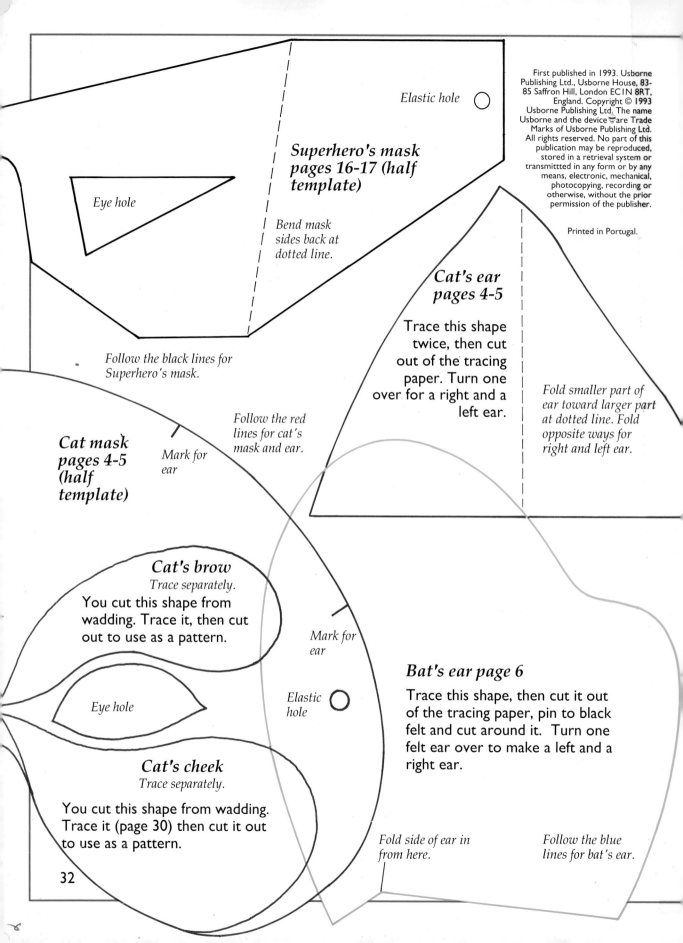

Elastic hole ◯

Superhero's mask pages 16-17 (half template)

Eye hole

Bend mask sides back at dotted line.

Follow the black lines for Superhero's mask.

Cat's ear pages 4-5

Trace this shape twice, then cut out of the tracing paper. Turn one over for a right and a left ear.

Fold smaller part of ear toward larger part at dotted line. Fold opposite ways for right and left ear.

Cat mask pages 4-5 (half template)

Mark for ear

Follow the red lines for cat's mask and ear.

Cat's brow
Trace separately.
You cut this shape from wadding. Trace it, then cut out to use as a pattern.

Eye hole

Mark for ear

Elastic hole ◯

Bat's ear page 6

Trace this shape, then cut it out of the tracing paper, pin to black felt and cut around it. Turn one felt ear over to make a left and a right ear.

Cat's cheek
Trace separately.

You cut this shape from wadding. Trace it (page 30) then cut it out to use as a pattern.

Fold side of ear in from here.

Follow the blue lines for bat's ear.